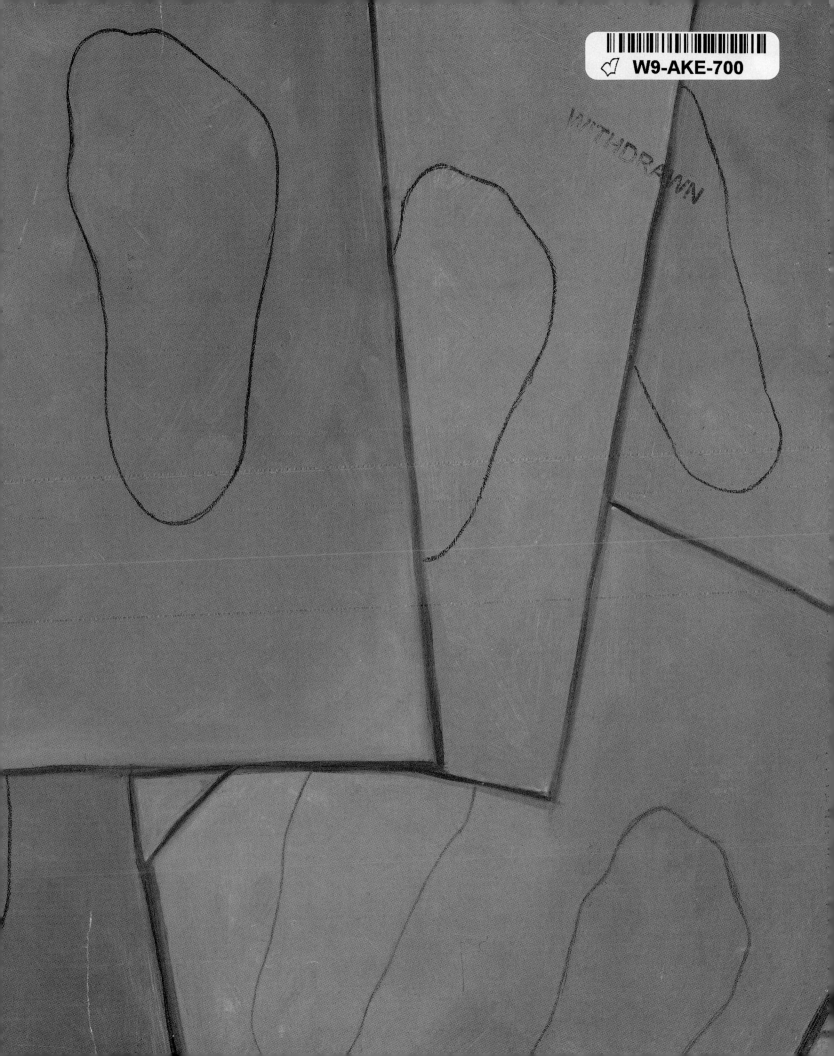

NEW SHOES

by Susan Lynn Meyer

illustrated by Eric Velasquez

Holiday House / New York

For Hannah—S. L. M.

For Walter Dean Myers—E. V.

I would like to thank Patty Bovie, Susan Lubner, and Beth Glass for reading many earlier drafts
of the manuscript, and Anita Hill for helping me understand what Mama would say to Ella Mae.
Thank-you to Sylvie Frank, who chose this story and believed in it,
and to Grace Maccarone, for shepherding this book into the world.
S. L. M.

Text copyright © 2015 by Susan Lynn Meyer
Illustrations copyright © 2015 by Eric Velasquez
All Rights Reserved
HOLIDAY HOUSE is registered in the U.S. Patent and Trademark Office.
Printed and Bound in October 2014 at Toppan Leefung, DongGuan City, China.
The artwork was created with mixed media and oil colors on watercolor paper.
www.holidayhouse.com
First Edition
1 3 5 7 9 10 8 6 4 2
Library of Congress Cataloging-in-Publication Data
Meyer, Susan, 1960-
New shoes / by Susan Lynn Meyer ; illustrated by Eric Velasquez. — 1st ed.
p. cm.
Summary: "In this historical fiction picture book, Ella Mae and her cousin Charlotte,
both African American, start their own shoe store when they learn that they cannot try on shoes
at the shoe store" — Provided by publisher.
ISBN 978-0-8234-2528-0 (hardcover)
[1. Discrimination—Fiction. 2. Segregation—Fiction.
3. African Americans—Fiction. 4. Shoes—Fiction.]
I. Velasquez, Eric, ill. II. Title.
PZ7.M571752Ne 2015
[E]—dc23
2012019673

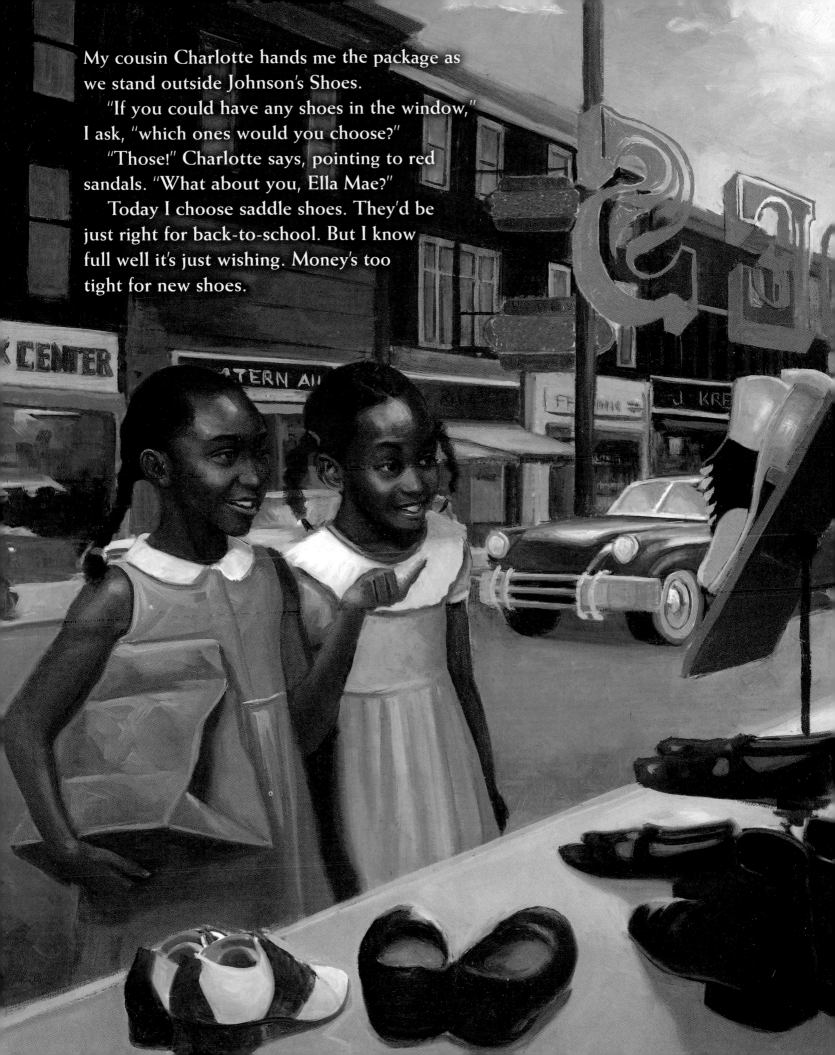

My cousin Charlotte hands me the package as we stand outside Johnson's Shoes.

"If you could have any shoes in the window," I ask, "which ones would you choose?"

"Those!" Charlotte says, pointing to red sandals. "What about you, Ella Mae?"

Today I choose saddle shoes. They'd be just right for back-to-school. But I know full well it's just wishing. Money's too tight for new shoes.

When I get home, Mama opens the package. "Winslow's shoes are in good shape!" she says. She hands them to my brother Clayton.

That's the way we always hand them down. Winslow's shoes go to Clayton, Charlotte's go to me. I clean Charlotte's old shoes. But when I put them on, they pinch my toes. I show Mama.

Mama sighs. "We'll just have to scrape together money for new shoes."

Shoes I pick out myself! I can't believe it! On Saturday we're going to Johnson's!

On Saturday morning when
we walk in, the bell jingles.
Mr. Johnson looks our way.
Behind us, the door jingles
again. A girl with yellow
curls walks in with her
daddy. Mr. Johnson heads
toward them.

Mama and I walk to the back of the store and stand against the wall. That blond-haired girl tries on shoes, posing in front of the mirror. I sigh. Weren't we here first? But I know colored people always have to wait.

Finally, the girl's daddy buys her a new pair of shoes, and they leave.

"How can I help you now?" Mr. Johnson says to us.
I point to a display of saddle shoes. "I want
to try those on, sir!" I say.

I hear Mama suck in her breath. "Oh, we'll
do something different, Ella Mae," she
says. "We'll make a picture of
your feet for Mr. Johnson."

"But . . . ," I start
to say.

"Pencil and paper are
over there, gal," Mr. Johnson
says to Mama.

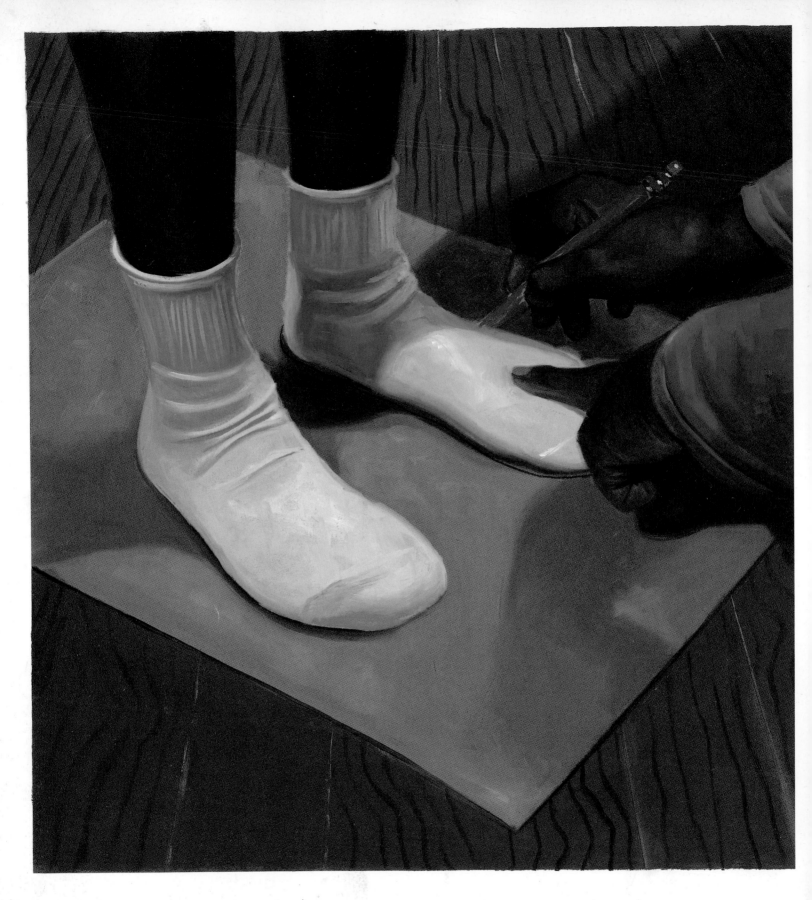

Mama traces my feet. Mr. Johnson takes the paper and comes back
with a shoe box.

Mama holds the shoes next to me. Mr. Johnson fidgets.

"Yes, I think these will fit," Mama says, and she counts out money.

Rain is pouring down when we leave. Mama snaps open her umbrella.
"Mama," I say, "Can't colored folks try on shoes?"
Mama sighs. "No." But then she puts on a smile. "Let's think about
how nice your feet will look for school."
I like my shoes. But it isn't fair that the other girl can try them on and
I can't. Mama and I walk on together, listening to the rain.

The next day in the school yard I show Charlotte
my shoes, but then I tell about what happened at
Johnson's.

Charlotte nods. "That's happened to me too," she
whispers.

Even though I have new shoes, I feel bad most of
the day.

But then during spelling I have an idea. I tell
Charlotte as we walk home.

"Yes!" she says. "I'll help!"

So Charlotte and I do chores.

We scrub, we pick the last green beans, we mind babies. Most folks say they can't pay much.

"Never mind," I say. "We'll work for a nickel and a pair of outgrown shoes."

At the end of the
month, we line up the
shoes on empty shelves
in the old barn next to
our house.

Charlotte scoops up
the coins. "I'll go buy
the polish!" she says.

While she is gone, I clean the shoes
with soft rags, then I pull out all the
dirty shoelaces. I wash them in lots
of soapy water until the water
squeezes off them clean.
I hang the laces on the
clothesline to dry in
the sun.

Charlotte comes running back.
"I call red!" she says.

She uses a nickel to pry open the red tin, and I open the black. I take a pair of shoes and rub the polish in. Then I scrunch up my hand inside, smoothing out all the wrinkles, and buff the shoes until they shine.

The sun has dried the laces now. I thread them back through the holes.

Charlotte holds up the shiny red Mary Jane she has been buffing. "Almost as good as new!" she says proudly.

The neighbors know we are ready to open even before
the paint on our sign is dry. "Ella Mae and Charlotte's Shoes,"
it says. "Price—10¢ and another used pair."

Mrs. Douglass peeps in the barn door
holding little Laura's hand. Right
behind them I see more
neighbors coming.

"Look at this!" Mrs. Douglass marvels. "No need to go to Johnson's now!"
Then she hesitates. "Last time the shoes from Johnson's gave my Laura
blisters," she says. "Can she try these on to see which ones fit best?"
Charlotte and I smile. We hold our heads up proud.

"Yes, ma'am, she can,"
I say loud and clear.
"In our store, anyone
who walks in the door
can try on all the shoes
they want."

AUTHOR'S NOTE

Ella Mae is a fictional character. But the discrimination that she faces was very real. Until the mid-1960s, many places in America had laws and traditions, known as Jim Crow or segregation, that were unjust to African Americans. Segregation was especially strong in the South, but it could be found throughout the United States.

Under Jim Crow, black citizens were often prevented from voting. In many places, black children had to go to separate schools from white children. The schools were supposed to be "separate but equal," but in reality the schools set aside for black children were more crowded and run-down than those white children attended. Blacks had to sit in the back of public buses and trains. Sometimes, if the seats for whites were full, blacks had to give up their seats to whites. Blacks had to use separate bathrooms and water fountains. Many lunch counters and restaurants would not serve African Americans. In stores, African Americans often had to wait until all white customers had been served. And African Americans were not permitted to try on clothes, hats, or shoes.

But as Ella Mae and Charlotte do, African Americans found ways of fighting back against the unfair system. For example, some people decided never to spend money at a restaurant that would only serve them by handing food out the back door. People also came together and organized to fight for justice. This struggle came to be called the civil rights movement. In 1964, the Civil Rights Act made it illegal to discriminate against people because of their race, color, sex, religion, or national origin. The Voting Rights Act, passed in 1965, protected the right of African Americans to register and to vote.

A note about the language: this story is set in the 1950s, so Ella Mae describes herself as "colored." But language changes over time, and today she would describe herself as "black" or "African American."